2000

JANUARY

S	M	T	W	T	F	S
						1
2	3	4	5	6	7	8
9	10	11	12	13	14	15
16	17	18	19	20	21	22
23	24	25	26	27	28	29
30	31					

FEBRUARY

S	M	T	W	T	F	S
		1	2	3	4	5
6	7	8	9	10	11	12
13	14	15	16	17	18	19
20	21	22	23	24	25	26
27	28	29				

MARCH

S	M	T	W	T	F	S
						4
						11
12	13	14	15	16	17	18
19	20	21	22	23	24	25
26	27	28	29	30	31	

APRIL

S	M	T	W	T	F	S
						1
2	3	4	5	6	7	8
9	10	11	12	13	14	15
16	17	18	19	20	21	22
23	24	25	26	27	28	29
30						

MAY

S	M	T	W	T	F	S
	1	2	3	4	5	6
7	8	9	10	11	12	13
14	15	16	17	18	19	20
21	22	23	24	25	26	27
28	29	30	31			

JUNE

S	M	T	W	T	F	S
				1	2	3
4	5	6	7	8	9	10
11	12	13	14	15	16	17
18	19	20	21	22	23	24
25	26	27	28	29	30	

JULY

S	M	T	W	T	F	S
						1
2	3	4	5	6	7	8
9	10	11	12	13	14	15
16	17	18	19	20	21	22
23	24	25	26	27	28	29
30	31					

AUGUST

S	M	T	W	T	F	S
		1	2	3	4	5
6	7	8	9	10	11	12
13	14	15	16	17	18	19
20	21	22	23	24	25	26
27	28	29	30	31		

SEPTEMBER

S	M	T	W	T	F	S
					1	2
3	4	5	6	7	8	9
10	11	12	13	14	15	16
17	18	19	20	21	22	23
24	25	26	27	28	29	30

OCTOBER

S	M	T	W	T	F	S
1	2	3	4	5	6	7
8	9	10	11	12	13	14
15	16	17	18	19	20	21
22	23	24	25	26	27	28
29	30	31				

NOVEMBER

S	M	T	W	T	F	S
			1	2	3	4
5	6	7	8	9	10	11
12	13	14	15	16	17	18
19	20	21	22	23	24	25
26	27	28	29	30		

DECEMBER

S	M	T	W	T	F	S
					1	2
3	4	5	6	7	8	9
10	11	12	13	14	15	16
17	18	19	20	21	22	23
24	25	26	27	28	29	30
31						

PERSONAL NOTES

Name ....

Address ....

....

....

....

Telephone (private) ....

Telephone (business) ....

Telephone (mobile) ....

Fax ....

E-mail ....

Notes ....

....

....

....

....

If this Diary is found, please return to the owner
at the above address

THE TOLKIEN DIARY 2000

ILLUSTRATED BY TED NASMITH

HarperCollins*Publishers*

HarperCollins*Publishers*
77-85 Fulham Palace Road
Hammersmith, London W6 8JB
www.**fire**and**water**.com

Published by HarperCollins*Publishers* 1999
The Tolkien Diary 2000
© HarperCollinsPublishers 1999

All illustrations © Ted Nasmith 1998, 1999
Additional drawings taken from *Pictures by J.R.R.
Tolkien*, © George Allen & Unwin (Publishers)
Ltd 1979

Quotations taken from *The Silmarillion*
© George Allen & Unwin (Publishers) Ltd 1977

 ® is a registered trademark of
The J.R.R.Tolkien Estate Limited

ISBN 0 261 10390 3

Printed and bound in Great Britain by
Scotprint Ltd, Musselburgh, Scotland

WORKS BY J.R.R. TOLKIEN

The Hobbit
Leaf by Niggle
On Fairy-Stories
Farmer Giles of Ham
The Homecoming of Beorhtnoth
The Lord of the Rings
The Adventures of Tom Bombadil
The Road Goes Ever On (with Donald Swann)
Smith of Wootton Major

WORKS PUBLISHED POSTHUMOUSLY

*Sir Gawain and the Green Knight, Pearl and
    Sir Orfeo*
The Father Christmas Letters
The Silmarillion
Pictures by J.R.R. Tolkien
Unfinished Tales
The Letters of J.R.R. Tolkien
Finn and Hengest
Mr Bliss
The Monsters and the Critics and Other Essays
Roverandom

THE HISTORY OF MIDDLE-EARTH
by Christopher Tolkien

I   The Book of Lost Tales, Part One
II   The Book of Lost Tales, Part Two
III   The Lays of Beleriand
IV   The Shaping of Middle-earth
V   The Lost Road and Other Writings
VI   The Return of the Shadow
VII   The Treason of Isengard
VIII   The War of the Ring
IX   Sauron Defeated
X   Morgoth's Ring
XI   The War of the Jewels
XII   The Peoples of Middle-earth

The Silmarillion

The illustrations in this year's Tolkien Diary are based on the tales of *The Silmarillion,* the underlying inspiration and source of J.R.R. Tolkien's imaginative writing. Long preceding in its origins *The Lord of the Rings*, it is the story of the First Age of Tolkien's world, the ancient drama to which characters in *The Lord of the Rings* look back, and in which some of them, such as Elrond and Galadriel, took part.

The title *Silmarillion* is shortened from *Quenta Silmarillion*, 'The History of the Silmarils', the three great jewels created by Fëanor, most gifted of the Elves, in which he imprisoned the light of the Two Trees that illuminated Valinor, the land of the gods. When Morgoth, the first Dark Lord, destroyed the trees, that light lived on only in the Silmarils; and Morgoth seized them and set them in his crown, guarded in the impenetrable fortress of Angband in the north of Middle-earth. *The Silmarillion* is the history of the rebellion of Fëanor and his people against the gods, their exile in Middle-earth, and their war, hopeless despite all the heroism of Elves and Men, against the great Enemy.

Though J.R.R. Tolkien worked on *The Silmarillion* throughout his life, he died before he was able to bring it to a final form, leaving his youngest son, Christopher, to prepare the work for publication. *The Silmarillion* was finally published on 15th September 1977. The book includes several other shorter works beside *The Silmarillion* proper. Preceding it are the *Ainulindalë* or Music of the Ainur, the myth of Creation, and the *Valaquenta*, in which the nature and powers of each of the gods are described. After *The Silmarillion* is the *Akallabêth*, the story of the downfall of the great island kingdom of Númenor at the end of the Second Age; and completing the volume is *Of the Rings of Power*, the tale of the great events at the end of the Third Age which form the basis of the epic *The Lord of the Rings*.

J.R.R. Tolkien

John Ronald Reuel Tolkien was born on 3rd January 1892 in Bloemfontein in the Orange Free State. He was educated at King Edward's School, Birmingham, where he began to develop his linguistic talent.

1914 saw the outbreak of the First World War. Ronald graduated the following year with a First in English language and literature at Oxford. Before embarking for France in 1916, he married his childhood sweetheart, Edith Bratt. He survived the Battle of the Somme but was later invalided home.

After the war Tolkien became Professor of Anglo-Saxon at Oxford. He had already started writing the great cycle of myths that became *The Silmarillion*. He and Edith had four children and it was for them that he first told the tale of *The Hobbit*, which was published in 1937. It was so successful that the publishers immediately wanted a sequel, but it was not until 1954 that the first volume of his great masterpiece, *The Lord of the Rings*, appeared. Its enormous popularity took Tolkien by surprise.

After retirement, Ronald and Edith Tolkien moved to Bournemouth, where Edith died in 1971. Tolkien died after a brief illness on 2nd September 1973.

Ted Nasmith

A native of Goderich, Ontario, Ted Nasmith spent much of his young life on the move and lived for three years in France. An artist prodigy, his talents were nurtured throughout his early years. He was introduced to J.R.R. Tolkien's works as a teenager and has been illustrating his literature ever since.

Now, in addition to his career as an architectural renderer, Ted has established himself as a renowned Tolkien interpreter. He had illustrated three Tolkien Calendars before *The Silmarillion*, representing for him a dream fulfilled. This diary contains a selection of paintings from that volume, plus six completely new pictures created specially for the 2000 diary and calendar.

JANUARY

Tuor, Gelmir and Arminas

Then Tuor followed the Noldor down the steps and waded in the cold water, until they passed into the shadow beyond the arch of stone. And then Gelmir brought forth one of those lamps for which the Noldor were renowned; for they were made of old in Valinor, and neither wind nor water could quench them, and when they were unhooded they sent forth a clear blue light from a flame imprisoned in white crystal. Now by the light that Gelmir held above his head Tuor saw that the river began to go suddenly down a smooth slope into a great tunnel, but beside its rock-hewn course there ran long flights of steps leading on and downward into a deep gloom beyond the beam of the lamp.

DECEMBER

| MONDAY 27 | TUESDAY 28 | WEDNESDAY 29 | THURSDAY 30 |

Weeks 0 - 1

FRIDAY 31
Millennium Holiday (UK)

SATURDAY 1
New Year's Day

SUNDAY 2

DECEMBER

S	M	T	W	T	F	S
				1	2	3	4
5	6	7	8	9	10	11
12	13	14	15	16	17	18
19	20	21	22	23	24	25
26	27	28	29	30	31	

MONDAY 3
New Year's Day Holiday (UK)

TUESDAY 4

WEDNESDAY 5

THURSDAY 6
Epiphany

FRIDAY 7

SATURDAY 8

SUNDAY 9

JANUARY

S	M	T	W	T	F	S
						1
2	3	4	5	6	7	8
9	10	11	12	13	14	15
16	17	18	19	20	21	22
23	24	25	26	27	28	29
30	31					

JANUARY

MONDAY 10   **TUESDAY 11**   **WEDNESDAY 12**   **THURSDAY 13**

Weeks 2 - 3

FRIDAY 14   **SATURDAY 15**   **SUNDAY 16**

JANUARY

S	M	T	W	T	F	S
						1
2	3	4	5	6	7	8
9	10	11	12	13	14	15
16	17	18	19	20	21	22
23	24	25	26	27	28	29
30	31					

MONDAY 17
Martin Luther King, Jr. Day (US)

TUESDAY 18

WEDNESDAY 19

THURSDAY 20

FRIDAY 21

SATURDAY 22

SUNDAY 23

JANUARY

S	M	T	W	T	F	S
						1
2	3	4	5	6	7	8
9	10	11	12	13	14	15
16	17	18	19	20	21	22
23	24	25	26	27	28	29
30	31					

MONDAY 24

TUESDAY 25

WEDNESDAY 26
Australia Day (Aus)

THURSDAY 27

Weeks 4 - 5

FRIDAY 28

SATURDAY 29

SUNDAY 30

JANUARY

S	M	T	W	T	F	S
						1
2	3	4	5	6	7	8
9	10	11	12	13	14	15
16	17	18	19	20	21	22
23	24	25	26	27	28	29
30	31					

MONDAY 31

TUESDAY 1

WEDNESDAY 2

THURSDAY 3

FRIDAY 4

SATURDAY 5
Chinese New Year

SUNDAY 6
Waitangi Day (NZ)

FEBRUARY

S	M	T	W	T	F	S
		1	2	3	4	5
6	7	8	9	10	11	12
13	14	15	16	17	18	19
20	21	22	23	24	25	26
27	28	29				

FEBRUARY

The Incoming Sea at the Rainbow Cleft

Now Tuor went on once more, seeking the gulls, high above the river; and as he went the sides of the ravine drew together again, and he came to a narrow channel, and it was filled with a great noise of water. And looking down Tuor saw a great marvel, as it seemed to him; for a wild flood came up the narrows and strove with the river that would still press on, and a wave like a wall rose up almost to the cliff-top, crowned with foam-crests flying in the wind. Then the river was thrust back, and the incoming flood swept roaring up the channel, drowning it in deep water, and the rolling of the boulders was like thunder as it passed. Thus Tuor was saved by the call of the sea-birds from death in the rising tide; and that was very great because of the season of the year and of the high wind from the sea.

FEBRUARY

MONDAY 7

TUESDAY 8

WEDNESDAY 9

THURSDAY 10

Weeks 6 - 7

FRIDAY 11

SATURDAY 12

SUNDAY 13

FEBRUARY

S	M	T	W	T	F	S
		1	2	3	4	5
6	7	8	9	10	11	12
13	14	15	16	17	18	19
20	21	22	23	24	25	26
27	28	29				

MONDAY 14
St Valentine's Day

TUESDAY 15

WEDNESDAY 16

THURSDAY 17

FRIDAY 18

SATURDAY 19

SUNDAY 20

FEBRUARY

S	M	T	W	T	F	S
		1	2	3	4	5
6	7	8	9	10	11	12
13	14	15	16	17	18	19
20	21	22	23	24	25	26
27	28	29				

 FEBRUARY

MONDAY 21
Presidents' Day (US)

TUESDAY 22

WEDNESDAY 23

THURSDAY 24

Weeks 8 - 9

FRIDAY 25

SATURDAY 26

SUNDAY 27

FEBRUARY

S	M	T	W	T	F	S
		1	2	3	4	5
6	7	8	9	10	11	12
13	14	15	16	17	18	19
20	21	22	23	24	25	26
27	28	29				

MONDAY 28

TUESDAY 29

WEDNESDAY 1
St David's Day (Wales)

THURSDAY 2

FRIDAY 3

SATURDAY 4

SUNDAY 5

march

S	M	T	W	T	F	S
			1	2	3	4
5	6	7	8	9	10	11
12	13	14	15	16	17	18
19	20	21	22	23	24	25
26	27	28	29	30	31	

March

Illuin, Lamp of the Valar

In that time the Valar brought order to the seas and the lands and the mountains, and Yavanna planted at last the seeds that she had long devised. And since, when the fires were subdued or buried beneath the primeval hills, there was need of light, Aulë at the prayer of Yavanna wrought two mighty lamps for the lighting of the Middle-earth which he had built amid the encircling seas. Then Varda filled the lamps and Manwë hallowed them, and the Valar set them upon high pillars, more lofty than are any mountains of the later days. One lamp they raised near to the north of Middle-earth, and it was named Illuin; and the other was raised in the south, and it was named Ormal; and the light of the Lamps of the Valar flowed out over the Earth, so that all was lit as it were in a changeless day.

Then the seeds that Yavanna had sown began swiftly to sprout and to burgeon, and there arose a multitude of growing things great and small, mosses and grasses and great ferns, and trees whose tops were crowned with cloud as they were living mountains, but whose feet were wrapped in a green twilight.

march

MONDAY 6

TUESDAY 7

WEDNESDAY 8
Ash Wednesday

THURSDAY 9

Weeks 10 - 11

FRIDAY 10

SATURDAY 11

SUNDAY 12

march

S	M	T	W	T	F	S
			1	2	3	4
5	6	7	8	9	10	11
12	13	14	15	16	17	18
19	20	21	22	23	24	25
26	27	28	29	30	31	

MONDAY 13
Commonwealth Day

TUESDAY 14

WEDNESDAY 15

THURSDAY 16

FRIDAY 17
St Patrick's Day Holiday (Ireland)

SATURDAY 18

SUNDAY 19

MARCH

S	M	T	W	T	F	S
			1	2	3	4
5	6	7	8	9	10	11
12	13	14	15	16	17	18
19	20	21	22	23	24	25
26	27	28	29	30	31	

march

MONDAY 20
Vernal Equinox

TUESDAY 21
Human Rights' Day (South Africa)

WEDNESDAY 22

THURSDAY 23

Weeks 12 - 13

FRIDAY 24

SATURDAY 25

SUNDAY 26
British Summer Time begins

march

S	M	T	W	T	F	S
			1	2	3	4
5	6	7	8	9	10	11
12	13	14	15	16	17	18
19	20	21	22	23	24	25
26	27	28	29	30	31	

MONDAY 27	TUESDAY 28	WEDNESDAY 29	THURSDAY 30

FRIDAY 31	SATURDAY 1	SUNDAY 2	
		Mothering Sunday (UK)	

APRIL

S	M	T	W	T	F	S
						1
2	3	4	5	6	7	8
9	10	11	12	13	14	15
16	17	18	19	20	21	22
23	24	25	26	27	28	29
30						

APRIL

At Lake Cuiviénen

It is told that even as Varda ended her labours, and they were long, when first Menelmacar strode up the sky and the blue fire of Helluin flickered in the mists above the borders of the world, in that hour the Children of the Earth awoke, the Firstborn of Illúvatar. By the starlit mere of Cuiviénen, Water of Awakening, they rose from the sleep of Illúvatar; and while they dwelt yet silent by Cuiviénen their eyes beheld first of all things the stars of heaven. Therefore they have ever loved the starlight, and have revered Varda Elentári above all the Valar.

APRIL

MONDAY 3

TUESDAY 4

WEDNESDAY 5

THURSDAY 6

Weeks 14 - 15

FRIDAY 7

SATURDAY 8

SUNDAY 9

APRIL

S	M	T	W	T	F	S
						1
2	3	4	5	6	7	8
9	10	11	12	13	14	15
16	17	18	19	20	21	22
23	24	25	26	27	28	29
30						

MONDAY 10

TUESDAY 11

WEDNESDAY 12

THURSDAY 13

FRIDAY 14

SATURDAY 15

SUNDAY 16
Palm Sunday

APRIL

S	M	T	W	T	F	S
						1
2	3	4	5	6	7	8
9	10	11	12	13	14	15
16	17	18	19	20	21	22
23	24	25	26	27	28	29
30						

 # April

MONDAY 17

TUESDAY 18

WEDNESDAY 19

THURSDAY 20
First Day of Passover

Weeks 16 - 17

FRIDAY 21
Good Friday

SATURDAY 22

SUNDAY 23
Easter Sunday
St George's Day (England)

April

S	M	T	W	T	F	S
						1
2	3	4	5	6	7	8
9	10	11	12	13	14	15
16	17	18	19	20	21	22
23	24	25	26	27	28	29
30						

MONDAY 24
Easter Monday
Family Day (South Africa)

TUESDAY 25
Anzac Day (Aus/NZ)

WEDNESDAY 26

THURSDAY 27
Last Day of Passover
Freedom Day (South Africa)

FRIDAY 28

SATURDAY 29

SUNDAY 30

april

S	M	T	W	T	F	S
						1
2	3	4	5	6	7	8
9	10	11	12	13	14	15
16	17	18	19	20	21	22
23	24	25	26	27	28	29
30						

MAY

Lúthien Escapes the Treehouse

It is told in the Lay of Leithian how she escaped from the house in Hírilorn; for she put forth her arts of enchantment, and caused her hair to grow to great length, and of it she wove a dark robe that wrapped her beauty like a shadow, and it was laden with a spell of sleep. Of the strands that remained she twined a rope, and she let it down from her window; and as the end swayed above the guards that sat beneath the tree they fell into a deep slumber. Then Lúthien climbed from her prison, and shrouded in her shadowy cloak she escaped from all eyes, and vanished out of Doriath.

 **MAY**

MONDAY 1
May Day Holiday (UK & Rep. of Ireland)
Workers' Day (South Africa)

TUESDAY 2

WEDNESDAY 3

THURSDAY 4

Weeks 18 - 19

FRIDAY 5

SATURDAY 6

SUNDAY 7

MAY

S	M	T	W	T	F	S
	1	2	3	4	5	6
7	8	9	10	11	12	13
14	15	16	17	18	19	20
21	22	23	24	25	26	27
28	29	30	31			

MONDAY 8

TUESDAY 9

WEDNESDAY 10

THURSDAY 11

FRIDAY 12

SATURDAY 13

SUNDAY 14
Mother's Day (US & Can)

MAY

S	M	T	W	T	F	S
	1	2	3	4	5	6
7	8	9	10	11	12	13
14	15	16	17	18	19	20
21	22	23	24	25	26	27
28	29	30	31			

 **MAY**

MONDAY 15
Victoria Day (Can)

TUESDAY 16

WEDNESDAY 17

THURSDAY 18

Weeks 20 - 21

FRIDAY 19

SATURDAY 20

SUNDAY 21

MAY

S	M	T	W	T	F	S
	1	2	3	4	5	6
7	8	9	10	11	12	13
14	15	16	17	18	19	20
21	22	23	24	25	26	27
28	29	30	31			

MONDAY 22

TUESDAY 23

WEDNESDAY 24

THURSDAY 25

FRIDAY 26

SATURDAY 27

SUNDAY 28

MAY

S	M	T	W	T	F	S
	1	2	3	4	5	6
7	8	9	10	11	12	13
14	15	16	17	18	19	20
21	22	23	24	25	26	27
28	29	30	31			

JUNE

Beren and Lúthien are Flown to Safety

Then they lifted up Lúthien and Beren from the earth, and bore them aloft into the clouds. Below them suddenly thunder rolled, lightnings leaped upward, and the mountains quaked. Fire and smoke belched forth from Thangorodrim, and flaming bolts were hurled far abroad, falling ruinous upon the lands; and the Noldor in Hithlum trembled. But Thorondor took his way far above the earth, seeking the high roads of heaven, where the sun daylong shines unveiled and the moon walks amid the cloudless stars. Thus they passed swiftly over Dor-nu-Fauglith, and over Taur-nu-Fuin, and came above the hidden valley of Tumladen. No cloud nor mist lay there, and looking down Lúthien saw far below, as a white light starting from a green jewel, the radiance of Gondolin the fair where Turgon dwelt. But she wept, for she thought that Beren would surely die; he spoke no word, nor opened his eyes, and knew thereafter nothing of his flight.

 **MAY**

MONDAY 29
Memorial Day (Observed) (US)
Spring Bank Holiday (UK)

TUESDAY 30

WEDNESDAY 31

THURSDAY 1

Weeks 22 - 23

FRIDAY 2

SATURDAY 3

SUNDAY 4

MAY

S	M	T	W	T	F	S
		1	2	3	4	5	6
7	8	9	10	11	12	13
14	15	16	17	18	19	20
21	22	23	24	25	26	27
28	29	30	31			

MONDAY 5
Holiday (Rep. of Ireland)
Queen's Birthday (Aus/NZ)

TUESDAY 6

WEDNESDAY 7

THURSDAY 8

FRIDAY 9

SATURDAY 10

SUNDAY 11

JUNE

S	M	T	W	T	F	S
				1	2	3
4	5	6	7	8	9	10
11	12	13	14	15	16	17
18	19	20	21	22	23	24
25	26	27	28	29	30	

JUNE

MONDAY 12

TUESDAY 13

WEDNESDAY 14

THURSDAY 15

Weeks 24 - 25

FRIDAY 16
Youth Day (South Africa)

SATURDAY 17

SUNDAY 18
Father's Day (UK & US)

JUNE

S	M	T	W	T	F	S
				1	2	3
4	5	6	7	8	9	10
11	12	13	14	15	16	17
18	19	20	21	22	23	24
25	26	27	28	29	30	

MONDAY 19

TUESDAY 20

WEDNESDAY 21
Summer Solstice

THURSDAY 22

FRIDAY 23

SATURDAY 24
St Jean Baptiste Day (Quebec)

SUNDAY 25

JUNE

S	M	T	W	T	F	S
				1	2	3
4	5	6	7	8	9	10
11	12	13	14	15	16	17
18	19	20	21	22	23	24
25	26	27	28	29	30	

JULY

Fingon and Gothmog

But now in the western battle Fingon and Turgon were assailed by a tide of foes thrice greater than all the force that was left to them. Gothmog, Lord of Balrogs, high-captain of Angband, was come; and he drove a dark wedge between the Elvenhosts, surrounding King Fingon, and thrusting Turgon and Húrin aside towards the Fen of Serech. Then he turned upon Fingon. That was a grim meeting. At last Fingon stood alone with his guard dead about him; and he fought with Gothmog, until another Balrog came behind and cast a thong of fire about him. Then Gothmog hewed him with his black axe, and a white flame sprang up from the helm of Fingon as it was cloven. Thus fell the High King of the Noldor.

JUNE

MONDAY 26

TUESDAY 27

WEDNESDAY 28

THURSDAY 29

Weeks 26 - 27

FRIDAY 30

SATURDAY 1
Canada Day (Canada)

SUNDAY 2

JUNE

S	M	T	W	T	F	S
				1	2	3
4	5	6	7	8	9	10
11	12	13	14	15	16	17
18	19	20	21	22	23	24
25	26	27	28	29	30	

JULY

MONDAY 3

TUESDAY 4
Independence Day (US)

WEDNESDAY 5

THURSDAY 6

FRIDAY 7

SATURDAY 8

SUNDAY 9

JULY

S	M	T	W	T	F	S
						1
2	3	4	5	6	7	8
9	10	11	12	13	14	15
16	17	18	19	20	21	22
23	24	25	26	27	28	29
30	31					

JULY

MONDAY 10

TUESDAY 11

WEDNESDAY 12
Battle of the Boyne Holiday (N. Ireland)

THURSDAY 13

Weeks 28 - 29

FRIDAY 14

SATURDAY 15

SUNDAY 16

JULY

S	M	T	W	T	F	S
						1
2	3	4	5	6	7	8
9	10	11	12	13	14	15
16	17	18	19	20	21	22
23	24	25	26	27	28	29
30	31					

MONDAY 17

TUESDAY 18

WEDNESDAY 19

THURSDAY 20

FRIDAY 21

SATURDAY 22

SUNDAY 23

JULY

S	M	T	W	T	F	S
						1
2	3	4	5	6	7	8
9	10	11	12	13	14	15
16	17	18	19	20	21	22
23	24	25	26	27	28	29
30	31					

 # july

MONDAY 24

TUESDAY 25

WEDNESDAY 26

THURSDAY 27

Weeks 30 - 31

FRIDAY 28

SATURDAY 29

SUNDAY 30

july

S	M	T	W	T	F	S
						1
2	3	4	5	6	7	8
9	10	11	12	13	14	15
16	17	18	19	20	21	22
23	24	25	26	27	28	29
30	31					

MONDAY 31

TUESDAY 1

WEDNESDAY 2

THURSDAY 3

FRIDAY 4

SATURDAY 5

SUNDAY 6

AUGUST

S	M	T	W	T	F	S
		1	2	3	4	5
6	7	8	9	10	11	12
13	14	15	16	17	18	19
20	21	22	23	24	25	26
27	28	29	30	31		

AUGUST

Beleg is Slain

Then he was aroused into a sudden wakefulness of rage and fear, and seeing one bending over him with naked blade he leapt up with a great cry, believing that Orcs were come again to torment him; and grappling with him in the darkness he seized Anglachel, and slew Beleg Cúthalion thinking him a foe.

But as he stood, finding himself free, and ready to sell his life dearly against imagined foes, there came a great flash of lightning above them; and in its light he looked down on Beleg's face. Then Túrin stood stonestill and silent, staring on that dreadful death, knowing what he had done.

AUGUST

MONDAY 7
August Holiday (Scotland & Rep. of Ireland)
Civic Holiday (Canada)

TUESDAY 8

WEDNESDAY 9
National Women's Day (South Africa)

THURSDAY 10

Weeks 32 - 33

FRIDAY 11

SATURDAY 12

SUNDAY 13

AUGUST

S	M	T	W	T	F	S
		1	2	3	4	5
6	7	8	9	10	11	12
13	14	15	16	17	18	19
20	21	22	23	24	25	26
27	28	29	30	31		

MONDAY 14	TUESDAY 15	WEDNESDAY 16	THURSDAY 17

| FRIDAY 18 | SATURDAY 19 | SUNDAY 20 | |

AUGUST

S	M	T	W	T	F	S
		1	2	3	4	5
6	7	8	9	10	11	12
13	14	15	16	17	18	19
20	21	22	23	24	25	26
27	28	29	30	31		

AUGUST

MONDAY 21

TUESDAY 22

WEDNESDAY 23

THURSDAY 24

Weeks 34 - 35

FRIDAY 25

SATURDAY 26

SUNDAY 27

AUGUST

S	M	T	W	T	F	S
		1	2	3	4	5
6	7	8	9	10	11	12
13	14	15	16	17	18	19
20	21	22	23	24	25	26
27	28	29	30	31		

MONDAY 28
Summer Bank Holiday (UK)

TUESDAY 29

WEDNESDAY 30

THURSDAY 31

FRIDAY 1

SATURDAY 2

SUNDAY 3

SEPTEMBER

S	M	T	W	T	F	S
					1	2
3	4	5	6	7	8	9
10	11	12	13	14	15	16
17	18	19	20	21	22	23
24	25	26	27	28	29	30

SEPTEMBER

Finduilas is Led Past Túrin
at the Sack of Nargothrond

And while he was yet held by the eyes of the dragon in torment of mind, and could not stir, the Orcs drove away the herded captives, and they passed nigh to Túrin and crossed over the bridge. Among them was Finduilas, and she cried out to Túrin as she went; but not until her cries and the wailing of the captives was lost upon the northward road did Glaurung release Túrin, and he might not stop his ears against the voice that haunted him after.

 SEPTEMBER

MONDAY 4
Labor Day (US & Canada)

TUESDAY 5

WEDNESDAY 6

THURSDAY 7

Weeks 36 - 37

FRIDAY 8

SATURDAY 9

SUNDAY 10

SEPTEMBER

S	M	T	W	T	F	S
					1	2
3	4	5	6	7	8	9
10	11	12	13	14	15	16
17	18	19	20	21	22	23
24	25	26	27	28	29	30

MONDAY 11

TUESDAY 12

WEDNESDAY 13

THURSDAY 14

FRIDAY 15

SATURDAY 16

SUNDAY 17

SEPTEMBER

S	M	T	W	T	F	S
					1	2
3	4	5	6	7	8	9
10	11	12	13	14	15	16
17	18	19	20	21	22	23
24	25	26	27	28	29	30

SEPTEMBER

MONDAY 18

TUESDAY 19

WEDNESDAY 20

THURSDAY 21

Weeks 38 - 39

FRIDAY 22
Autumnal Equinox

SATURDAY 23

SUNDAY 24
Heritage Day (South Africa)

SEPTEMBER

S	M	T	W	T	F	S
					1	2
3	4	5	6	7	8	9
10	11	12	13	14	15	16
17	18	19	20	21	22	23
24	25	26	27	28	29	30

MONDAY 25	TUESDAY 26	WEDNESDAY 27	THURSDAY 28

FRIDAY 29	SATURDAY 30	SUNDAY 1	
	Rosh Hashanah		

OCTOBER

S	M	T	W	T	F	S
1	2	3	4	5	6	7
8	9	10	11	12	13	14
15	16	17	18	19	20	21
22	23	24	25	26	27	28
29	30	31				

OCTOBER

The Slaying of Glaurung

Then Turambar summoned all his will and courage and climbed the cliff alone, and came beneath the dragon. Then he drew Gurthang, and with all the might of his arm, and of his hate, he thrust it into the soft belly of the Worm, even up to the hilts. But when Glaurung felt his death-pang, he screamed, and in his dreadful throe he heaved up his bulk and hurled himself across the chasm, and there lay lashing and coiling in his agony.

OCTOBER

MONDAY 2	TUESDAY 3	WEDNESDAY 4	THURSDAY 5

Weeks 40 - 41

	FRIDAY 6	SATURDAY 7	SUNDAY 8

OCTOBER

S	M	T	W	T	F	S
1	2	3	4	5	6	7
8	9	10	11	12	13	14
15	16	17	18	19	20	21
22	23	24	25	26	27	28
29	30	31				

MONDAY 9
Yom Kippur
Columbus Day (US)
Thanksgiving Day (Canada)

TUESDAY 10

WEDNESDAY 11

THURSDAY 12

FRIDAY 13

SATURDAY 14

SUNDAY 15

OCTOBER

S	M	T	W	T	F	S
1	2	3	4	5	6	7
8	9	10	11	12	13	14
15	16	17	18	19	20	21
22	23	24	25	26	27	28
29	30	31				

OCTOBER

MONDAY 16

TUESDAY 17

WEDNESDAY 18

THURSDAY 19

Weeks 42 - 43

FRIDAY 20

SATURDAY 21

SUNDAY 22

OCTOBER

S	M	T	W	T	F	S
1	2	3	4	5	6	7
8	9	10	11	12	13	14
15	16	17	18	19	20	21
22	23	24	25	26	27	28
29	30	31				

MONDAY 23
Labour Day (NZ)

TUESDAY 24

WEDNESDAY 25

THURSDAY 26

FRIDAY 27

SATURDAY 28

SUNDAY 29
British Summer Time ends

OCTOBER

S	M	T	W	T	F	S
1	2	3	4	5	6	7
8	9	10	11	12	13	14
15	16	17	18	19	20	21
22	23	24	25	26	27	28
29	30	31				

NOVEMBER

Ulmo Appears Before Tuor

Thus he came at length to the deserted halls of Vinyamar beneath Mount Taras, and he entered in, and found there the shield and hauberk, and the sword and helm, that Turgon had left there by the command of Ulmo long before; and he arrayed himself in those arms, and went down to the shore. But there came a great storm out of the west, and out of that storm Ulmo the Lord of waters arose in majesty and spoke to Tuor as he stood beside the sea. And Ulmo bade him depart from that place and seek out the hidden kingdom of Gondolin; and he gave Tuor a great cloak, to mantle him in shadow from the eyes of his enemies.

OCTOBER

MONDAY 30
Holiday (Rep. of Ireland)

TUESDAY 31
Hallowe'en

WEDNESDAY 1
All Saints' Day

THURSDAY 2

Weeks 44 - 45

FRIDAY 3

SATURDAY 4

SUNDAY 5

OCTOBER

S	M	T	W	T	F	S
1	2	3	4	5	6	7
8	9	10	11	12	13	14
15	16	17	18	19	20	21
22	23	24	25	26	27	28
29	30	31				

MONDAY 6

TUESDAY 7
Election Day (US)

WEDNESDAY 8

THURSDAY 9

FRIDAY 10

SATURDAY 11
Veterans' Day (US)
Remembrance Day (Canada)

SUNDAY 12
Remembrance Sunday (UK & Commonwealth)

NOVEMBER

S	M	T	W	T	F	S
			1	2	3	4
5	6	7	8	9	10	11
12	13	14	15	16	17	18
19	20	21	22	23	24	25
26	27	28	29	30		

NOVEMBER

MONDAY 13

TUESDAY 14

WEDNESDAY 15

THURSDAY 16

Weeks 46 - 47

FRIDAY 17

SATURDAY 18

SUNDAY 19

NOVEMBER

S	M	T	W	T	F	S
			1	2	3	4
5	6	7	8	9	10	11
12	13	14	15	16	17	18
19	20	21	22	23	24	25
26	27	28	29	30		

MONDAY 20

TUESDAY 21

WEDNESDAY 22

THURSDAY 23
Thanksgiving (US)

FRIDAY 24

SATURDAY 25

SUNDAY 26

NOVEMBER

S	M	T	W	T	F	S
			1	2	3	4
5	6	7	8	9	10	11
12	13	14	15	16	17	18
19	20	21	22	23	24	25
26	27	28	29	30		

December

Eärendil Searches Tirion

And he went up alone into the land, and came into the Calacirya, and it seemed to him empty and silent; for even as Morgoth and Ungoliant came in ages past, so now Eärendil had come at a time of festival, and wellnigh all the Elvenfolk were gone to Valimar, or were gathered in the halls of Manwë upon Taniquetil, and few were left to keep watch upon the walls of Tirion.

But some there were who saw him from afar, and the great light that he bore; and they went in haste to Valimar. But Eärendil climbed the green hill of Túna and found it bare; and he entered into the streets of Tirion, and they were empty; and his heart was heavy, for he feared that some evil had come even to the Blessed Realm. He walked in the deserted ways of Tirion, and the dust upon his raiment and his shoes was a dust of diamonds, and he shone and glistened as he climbed the long white stairs. And he called aloud in many tongues, both of Elves and Men, but there were none to answer him.

NOVEMBER

MONDAY 27

TUESDAY 28

WEDNESDAY 29

THURSDAY 30
St Andrew's Day (Scotland)

Weeks 48 - 49

FRIDAY 1

SATURDAY 2

SUNDAY 3

NOVEMBER

S	M	T	W	T	F	S
			1	2	3	4
5	6	7	8	9	10	11
12	13	14	15	16	17	18
19	20	21	22	23	24	25
26	27	28	29	30		

MONDAY 4

TUESDAY 5

WEDNESDAY 6

THURSDAY 7

FRIDAY 8

SATURDAY 9

SUNDAY 10

ðECEMBER

S	M	T	W	T	F	S
					1	2
3	4	5	6	7	8	9
10	11	12	13	14	15	16
17	18	19	20	21	22	23
24	25	26	27	28	29	30
31						

DECEMBER

MONDAY 11

TUESDAY 12

WEDNESDAY 13

THURSDAY 14

Weeks 50 - 51

FRIDAY 15

SATURDAY 16
Day of Reconciliation (South Africa)

SUNDAY 17

DECEMBER

S	M	T	W	T	F	S
					1	2
3	4	5	6	7	8	9
10	11	12	13	14	15	16
17	18	19	20	21	22	23
24	25	26	27	28	29	30
31						

MONDAY 18

TUESDAY 19

WEDNESDAY 20

THURSDAY 21
Winter Solstice

FRIDAY 22
First Day of Hanukkah

SATURDAY 23

SUNDAY 24

DECEMBER

S	M	T	W	T	F	S
					1	2
3	4	5	6	7	8	9
10	11	12	13	14	15	16
17	18	19	20	21	22	23
24	25	26	27	28	29	30
31						

DECEMBER

MONDAY 25
Christmas Day

TUESDAY 26
Boxing Day
St Stephen's Day (Rep. of Ireland)
Day of Goodwill (South Africa)

WEDNESDAY 27

THURSDAY 28

Weeks 52 - 53

FRIDAY 29

SATURDAY 30

SUNDAY 31

DECEMBER

S	M	T	W	T	F	S
					1	2
3	4	5	6	7	8	9
10	11	12	13	14	15	16
17	18	19	20	21	22	23
24	25	26	27	28	29	30
31						

JANUARY

MONDAY 1
New Year's Day

TUESDAY 2

WEDNESDAY 3

THURSDAY 4

FRIDAY 5

SATURDAY 6
Epiphany

SUNDAY 7

JANUARY

S	M	T	W	T	F	S
	1	2	3	4	5	6
7	8	9	10	11	12	13
14	15	16	17	18	19	20
21	22	23	24	25	26	27
28	29	30	31			

2001

Maglor Casts a Silmaril into the Sea

And it is told of Maglor that he could not endure the pain with which the Silmaril tormented him; and he cast it at last into the Sea, and thereafter he wandered ever upon the shores, singing in pain and regret beside the waves. For Maglor was mighty among the singers of old, named only after Daeron of Doriath; but he never came back among the people of the Elves. And thus it came to pass that the Silmarils found their long homes: one in the airs of heaven, and one in the fires of the heart of the world, and one in the deep waters.

NOTES & ADDRESSES

NOTES & ADDRESSES

NOTES & ADDRESSES

2000

JANUARY

S	M	T	W	T	F	S
						1
2	3	4	5	6	7	8
9	10	11	12	13	14	15
16	17	18	19	20	21	22
23	24	25	26	27	28	29
30	31					

FEBRUARY

S	M	T	W	T	F	S
		1	2	3	4	5
6	7	8	9	10	11	12
13	14	15	16	17	18	19
20	21	22	23	24	25	26
27	28	29				

MARCH

S	M	T	W	T	F	S
			1	2	3	4
5	6	7	8	9	10	11
12	13	14	15	16	17	18
19	20	21	22	23	24	25
26	27	28	29	30	31	

APRIL

S	M	T	W	T	F	S
						1
2	3	4	5	6	7	8
9	10	11	12	13	14	15
16	17	18	19	20	21	22
23	24	25	26	27	28	29
30						

MAY

S	M	T	W	T	F	S
	1	2	3	4	5	6
7	8	9	10	11	12	13
14	15	16	17	18	19	20
21	22	23	24	25	26	27
28	29	30	31			

JUNE

S	M	T	W	T	F	S
				1	2	3
4	5	6	7	8	9	10
11	12	13	14	15	16	17
18	19	20	21	22	23	24
25	26	27	28	29	30	

JULY

S	M	T	W	T	F	S
						1
2	3	4	5	6	7	8
9	10	11	12	13	14	15
16	17	18	19	20	21	22
23	24	25	26	27	28	29
30	31					

AUGUST

S	M	T	W	T	F	S
		1	2	3	4	5
6	7	8	9	10	11	12
13	14	15	16	17	18	19
20	21	22	23	24	25	26
27	28	29	30	31		

SEPTEMBER

S	M	T	W	T	F	S
					1	2
3	4	5	6	7	8	9
10	11	12	13	14	15	16
17	18	19	20	21	22	23
24	25	26	27	28	29	30

OCTOBER

S	M	T	W	T	F	S
1	2	3	4	5	6	7
8	9	10	11	12	13	14
15	16	17	18	19	20	21
22	23	24	25	26	27	28
29	30	31				

NOVEMBER

S	M	T	W	T	F	S
			1	2	3	4
5	6	7	8	9	10	11
12	13	14	15	16	17	18
19	20	21	22	23	24	25
26	27	28	29	30		

DECEMBER

S	M	T	W	T	F	S
					1	2
3	4	5	6	7	8	9
10	11	12	13	14	15	16
17	18	19	20	21	22	23
24	25	26	27	28	29	30
31						